Black
and
Bittern
Was Night

With bright, sweet thanks to Sheila, Tara, Yvette, star editors all — R.H.

To Mom and Dad — J.M.

Text © 2013 Robert Heidbreder
Illustrations © 2013 John Martz

Kids Can Press acknowledges the financial support of the Government of Ontario, through the Ontario Media Development Corporation's Ontario Book Initiative; the Ontario Arts Council; the Canada Council for the Arts; and the Government of Canada, through the CBF, for our publishing activity.

Published in Canada by
Kids Can Press Ltd.
25 Dockside Drive
Toronto, ON M5A 0B5

Published in the U.S. by
Kids Can Press Ltd.
2250 Military Road
Tonawanda, NY 14150

www.kidscanpress.com

The artwork in this book was rendered in Photoshop.
The text is set in Boudoir-Bold.

Edited by Yvette Ghione
Designed by Marie Bartholomew

This book is smyth sewn casebound.
Manufactured in Shenzhen, China, in 3/2013 through Asia Pacific Offset

CM 13 0 9 8 7 6 5 4 3 2 1

LIBRARY AND ARCHIVES CANADA CATALOGUING IN PUBLICATION

Heidbreder, Robert
     Black and bittern was night / written by Robert Heidbreder ;
illustrated by John Martz.

ISBN 978-1-55453-302-2

          I. Martz, John, 1978– II. Title.

PS8565.E42B53 2013   jC813'.54   C2011-900090-3

Kids Can Press is a *corus*™ Entertainment company

Black and Bittern Was Night

Robert Heidbreder
John Martz

Kids Can Press

Black and bittern was night,
that Halloween night,
when SKUL-A-MUG-MUGS
spled out skellety fright.

They ring-ruckled round,
enclupping the town,
with quake-quiver-up
and scree-scrackle down.

Then with scree-scrackle scroans
and fog-footed wheeze,
the SKUL-A-MUG-MUGS
splooed jaw-chawing freeze:

"We'll brain-frizz tall-bigs.
Halloween they'll deep nix.
They'll shup-clup inside
nasty Noras and Nicks!"

Loon-moon scoot-scatted
from thruffening clouds.
Hoot-holler whirrwind
quick-whipped up guffrouds.

Windows were shutterned,
tight-pulled all drapefolds.
Brain-frizzed tall-big ones
latch-click-locked doorholds.

"No trickery! No scrill-screes!
No dress spooks to streets!
On a SKUL-A-MUG night,
no Halloween treats!

"To bedmats and civverns
quick-splickety licks!"
screed splooked-out tall-bigs
to Noras and Nicks.

But of SKUL-A-MUG-MUGS
tyke-tots knew no scare.
"Outbrave them! Out SKUL them!"
they'd Halloween dare.

The quikstant they tot-took
and crish-crilled to beds,
fling-up again springsprung
ghost-civvered tyke heads.

Through crickcracks in doorholds
and see-throughs ajar,
steam-sped ghost-whist-hobs
from close-next and far.

They loud-crowded sidestalks,
flutflittering grugs,
scringing, twing-winging
to SKUL-A-MUG-MUGS:

"Thrickle! and thrackle!
Thinder-a-thray!
SKUL-A-MUG-MUGS,
we'll splook you away!"

Squik-quick as hair-scares
up-sprung SKUL-A-MUGS all,
hoarse-hollered-moan-groaned
their smeerk SKUL-A-MUG call:

"Drickle! and drackle!
Dead dinders and dreads!
Ghoulie-gob tykies,
we'll sceer off your heads!"

"To-fronten! To-backen!
Enclup SKULS right-tight,"
scrill-screed the tot-trickers.
"We'll full-face SKUL fright!"

Black-bittern night splintered
with SKUL-MUGS 'ginst tykes:
SKULS first to the fore,
then tots took their strikes.

The scare-fest crish-crashed,
up-over-round-under ...

... but strong-sure tyke-tots
out-movvered SKUL thunder.

Nip-swift child-tide
skit-skuttled their foes:
The SKUL-A-MUGS jellied
from top-tip to toes.

"Tough tyke-brats score win —
squik-foot out of town!"
the SKUL-A-MUGS screed,
creep-crawlied deep down.

A-bittern, defeated,
they skul-scled in scare,
leaving Halloween trick-treats
to tot-child do-dare.

While SKUL-A-MUG-MUGS
scled who-knows-which-where,
low drooped the howl-wind
as moonface out-pipped fair.

Then bonefroze tall-bigs
felt shakefrear fade 'way,
unlock-latched doorholds
to tricktreaters' play.

Ghost-civvered tot-tykes
glomgathered sweet-treats,
liff-laughing, flip-flapping
through SKUL-MUG-free streets.

With goodens aplenty,
yak-yawling with fun,
they cree-crickled home,
their SKUL-skirmish won!

Their ghost-civverns off,
in sweetens heap-deep,
they miggled with big-ones
of SKUL-A-MUG creep.

The tall-biggies quisted
how tot-tykes knew-true,
to skit-scare SKUL-MUGS
with splick derring-do?

But tot-tykes lip-grinned:
What knew they knew they.
Then they ghost-civved big-ones
and tune-taught the song's play.

One-all they sprang-sang,
ghost-hobbing up-down,
lip-looping that SKUL-MUGS
dip-drooped out of town:

"Thrickle! and thrackle!
Thinder-a-thray!
SKUL-A-MUG-MUGS,
we splooked you away ..."

Bright-long they cheer-chanted
that Halloween night,
how tot-tykes spled SKUL-MUGS
a black-bittern fright.